The Adventures of Jack & Adam

Jack & Adam

The Old Town

Anthony Broderick

Copyright © Anthony Broderick, 2018

First Published in Ireland, in 2018, in co-operation with
Choice Publishing, Drogheda, County Louth, Republic of Ireland.
www.choicepublishing.ie

Paperback ISBN: 978-1-911131-51-9
eBook ISBN: 978-1 911131-52-6

eBook ISBN: 978-1-911131-70-0 The Larry Right Series Episode 4

A CIP catalogue record for this book is available from
the National Library.

Introduction

Book four in *The Adventures of Jack and Adam series.* Jack and Adam go on holiday to a faraway destination. The boys are given some freedom to explore their surroundings. However, with freedom comes greater responsibility, as they are about to learn. It seems that some friendly faces that they encounter along the way have a hidden agenda. The brothers have to use the skills that they have acquired to try and solve a very serious problem.

Chapter 1 – Rookie Mistake

"Club still hasn't gotten used to that lampshade, has she?" joked Jack, as he turned around to hand Adam a washed plate.

"Can you ever get used to a lampshade stuck around your neck and throat?" replied Adam, sympathising with his dog. He thought about what it would be like if either he or his brother had to wear something like that around their necks all day.

However, lately both brothers felt like they had some large weights tied around their necks, as their lives had been all about washing and drying dishes, vacuuming the carpet in the hallway, cleaning the windows, not to mention preparing the dinners each and every afternoon. Jack looked like a bulldog chewing a wasp when he had to sit down and peel carrot after carrot and then move on to the parsnips.

The antics during the bonfire had given way to

an avalanche of punishment. Ironically enough, the only one to gain from that frightening night was Club. She had now put on at least a stone from comfort-eating and lack of exercise. It was amusing trying to play the odd game of fetch-the-ball with her, as she was barely able to pick up the ball because of her awkward head contraption.

Diamond, on the other hand, was like a first child watching her Mum and Dad direct all of their love and affection to a new-born baby. She had to scratch at the window to make sure Adam did not forget about her each morning. Some afternoons she would wander off down the field to get some insurance food, like a quick mouse or if she was lucky a few unsuspecting birds, to fill the hunger gap.

Dad told the boys to do all their jobs efficiently and not leave a morsel of food around when cleaning up. He hovered over Jack while he was cleaning the worktop area after the dishes were done, knowing well that if there was a short cut to take during any of these chores, Jack would take it.

"Not a problem!" Jack responded sarcastically, giving the sink and surroundings a quick rub before throwing the cloth down.

The boys' rooms had been their main habitats since the fire incident. They were only allowed outside occasionally and definitely did not want to disobey their parents again, mainly because in two days they would be going on holiday to the island of Gallibar.

Gallibar was a country that Adam was getting increasingly interested in. He had been looking at it in one of the new geography books that were on the sixth-class booklist. He was really intrigued by a place known as 'The Old Town' in the centre of Gallibar. The pages were covered in beautifully illustrated diagrams and maps, along with several interesting facts, and trivia questions at the bottom. Adam found it so easy to learn. If more books were like this there would be no need for a teacher, he pondered to himself, briefly imagining a strange world where learning was fun.

Jack, on the other hand, had struggled to keep himself sane in his room when all he could think about was going outside. He tried reading some books but it was futile. If his brain did not want to engage in education during school terms then it certainly would not function during the summer, when the sun beamed in through the unclosed curtains. However, he was applying himself to something constructive. He had created several drawings outlining a new type of slingshot. There had been a number of rooks pestering and annoying him with their constant cawing over on Mr Dott's property next door. They had a nest on top of one of the high oak trees and he felt it was his job to do something about this problem. His new design incorporated large elastic bands. He had saved these big bands after taking them out of his Dad's work trousers. Dad had pocketed the bands while fitting a dishwasher in a house. Jack found them extremely flexible and very durable, a perfect ingredient for a 'complete' slingshot.

"Bye bye, rook, you've make a mistake annoying me," Jack chirped. He eyed the two adult birds on the high branches next door with malice.

Mum was really enjoying her time off from all the housework. Putting her feet up each day, with her two sons busy as bees downstairs, she was on cloud nine. She even had time to take up a new hobby of walking. She now spent most of her mornings going for a walk with a friend through Willows Town and its surrounding roads. The two would walk briskly, gossiping about all the latest news and rumours that circulated in this close-knit area. They would normally pop in to get some meat for dinner from Mrs Slate on their way home.

Jack knew at this stage what time Mum would be coming back as that was his cue to jog downstairs and get ready to place the meat in the oven. Sometimes he contemplated deliberately burning the meat so he might not be asked to do the job again, but thought twice about it: another mistake before their holiday abroad could prove fatal.

Chapter 2 – Second Thoughts

"Come and give me a hand outside, boys!" Dad's voice was heard from downstairs.

The shout startled Adam a little, as he was so engrossed in his book, learning about capital cities. Jack only needed to be called once, placing his new weapon under his mattress before running down the stairs energetically. The boys knew that 'giving a hand' to their Dad meant some form of work outside.

"It's better than cutting turnips!" Adam turned and remarked to Jack as he met him at the back door.

Both brothers put on their working shoes and went out the back. It was a relief going outside and feeling the gentle breeze brush their faces, as the heat from the range inside was almost too much to handle.

Club slowly followed Dad down towards the shed, still suffering a little from the tiresome operation. Her now large bottom swayed from side to side as she strained her head to turn back and glance at the boys.

"Grab a handsaw from that shelf, Jack!" instructed Dad. He reeled up a large rope that lay on the cold concrete floor.

Jack asked his father what he was doing as he took the saw gently down and removed its safety cover.

"Mr Dott has been complaining about some of the high branches that are overhanging on his side of the wall. Today we have to do some chopping," he explained.

Wouldn't you know he would be complaining! As if we didn't have enough to worry about without having him create hassle again, thought Adam. He took another smaller handsaw down from a steel cabinet.

The three moved around to the back of the treehouse, passing by the area where one of the booby traps had been set earlier that summer. The dug-out pit had now been filled in. Jack felt it would be wiser not to have anyone else fall into it. Adam's mind reflected on the incident, seeing flashbacks of the large man's chin smashing off the side of the ground. He could still hear the loud buzz of the wasps as they sunk their stings into the bodies of both of the men. He hadn't slept for days after that event, wondering if those two men would come back and seek revenge. He and Jack had also decided not to mention any of what had happened to Mum or Dad, as they were already in enough trouble.

The boys placed their legs securely on a few low branches as they began climbing up the two large trees. Dad stayed at ground level, pointing the brothers in the right direction.

"Right about there, Jack!" Dad yelled as Jack held himself at the correct location to begin sawing the branch. In the same way Adam made himself secure, sitting back on one of the stronger branches before using the jagged blade to mark out the section of bark he was going to cut.

The view was stunning up this high, overlooking the surrounding countryside. Dark green bushes, light green fields and hundreds of yellow dandelions decorated the landscape.

Soon, however, the scenery changed for the worse as they spotted Mr Dott strolling down his garden, smirking from ear to ear. His whining voice was heard from across the wall instructing them not to miss any of the branches.

Wearing a tee-shirt that was far too big for him, Mr Dott stood staring up at the boys in the trees. Adam thought for a minute about replying to him but decided it wasn't worth the effort and that he probably should not get too distracted this high up off the ground.

"Don't get up to any mischief up there, boys. We would not like any more disasters to occur!" he said sarcastically, trying his best to be annoying.

Jack couldn't refrain from suggesting to Mr Dott that perhaps he should get his son, Ralf, to give them a hand, if he was not still 'studying for exams'. Adam bit his upper lip at this suggestion, trying not to laugh.

Dad gave a sharp look up to Jack: enough was enough. Mr Dott's face began to glow a little red, not wanting a young boy to get the better of him.

"Don't leave any branches on my lawn!" he responded in frustration. He then turned and moved slowly back up towards his house.

Dad smiled to himself as he signalled Adam to keep cutting the wide branch at the top. The boys used their strength to saw into the dry wood. Adam's section was very difficult to slice through, on account of several knots in the timber, not to mention the blunt teeth on the end of his saw. The sweat poured down Jack's brow as he sat back on the branch for a little breather.

He then noticed 'Mr Rook', one of the birds that had been on his eliminating list, perched with its chest out on the highest tree, on the far side of Mr Dott's. The bird was nestled cosily with a couple of other birds. To its left was a collection of little rooks gaping up towards their mother. Loud chirps echoed from their innocent little heads as they tried to get their mother's attention. As Jack took these images in, he began to think twice about harming any of these creatures. He did not want to see any young grow up without a mother or father.

Adam announced that he was nearly finished cutting the final branches. This area to the rear of the treehouse was very dense with trees.

When the branches were cut, they didn't exactly fall to the ground but rather rested on each other, sometimes hanging onto a tree beneath.

Dad's plan was to get Adam to tie a rope around a cut-off section and tug it down from the ground. Adam tied the knot and Dad pulled the rope, forcing it through the other leaves towards the lawn. As it hit the surface, Club gave it the once-over, sniffing it quickly up and down to get any strange scent or smells from it.

Jack looped the rope around his branch and soon there was nothing overhanging that Mr Dott could give out about. Dad was now going to turn this task into something positive, getting the electric chainsaw out from the shed to cut up the branches for firewood.

"And we thought the fire was hot today!" remarked Adam. He turned to his brother as he reached the ground. "Wait until these branches start burning, the range will be like a furnace!"

"Yes, and we will never get Diamond out of the house!" added Jack. He too jumped down onto the grass and walked with his saw back into the shed.

Chapter 3 – Bound For Gallibar

Two days passed and Jack and Adam definitely deserved a holiday. They had slaved away at home with job upon job and their behaviour had been second to none. Dad had burned through seven bags of sticks since cutting the overhanging branches down, and Jack and Adam were longing to dive into a nice cool swimming pool and escape this stuffy, clammy feeling inside. Jack had also gone with his instinct and allowed the annoying rook to stay nested in his tree and protect his family, for the time being.

It was now time to pack their bags and head off on a trip to the Old Town, Gallibar. Mum had noticed that Adam had been doing extremely well all year in geography at school and thought it would be a nice idea to travel abroad to experience the culture and scenery first-hand.

Adam walked into his brother's room to check

on his progress with packing. Jack did not take pride in packing but just threw in the first few things that popped out of his shelves and drawers. If it was up to him he would wear the same top and trousers every day, not having developed the fashion bug that some of his friends were acquiring at school.

Adam wondered if the weather would be as good in Gallibar as they all hoped, whilst deciding about how many pairs of shorts he should bring. Mum suggested that he should bring three pairs anyway. And one pair of trousers for if the weather cooled off at night.

The boys soon left their suitcases at the front door all ready for off, their passports and holiday money safely secured in their pockets, along with some chewy sweets for the flight.

Dad had invited over Jasmine to keep an eye on Club and Diamond. She had now finished all her music exams at college and would soon be looking for full-time employment. Dad outlined the feeding schedules along with play time each day. Club needed to be given some tablets twice daily as part of the recovery process from the operation, so making sure she completely swallowed them in her food would be Jasmine's most challenging task.

Club and Diamond knew Jasmine quite well and enjoyed when she came over to mind the boys. Jasmine smiled as she wished the family a safe trip, hoping that minding Club and Diamond would be a lot easier than keeping a constant eye on Jack and Adam.

"Now, are we sure we have brought everything?" inquired Mum. She raced back into the house for the third time, remembering something else.

"Yes! Yes we have!" Jack responded, just wanting to listen to a few good tunes on the radio on their long drive from Willows Town to the airport.

On arrival at Terminal 2, mayhem prevailed. It reminded the boys of some Wednesday nights at the auction. Everyone rushed and raced to print off their boarding passes, check in their bags and catch their flight. People young, middle-aged and old passed by as the family followed their queue to check in their four suitcases at the departure desk.

Jack noticed an unoccupied pool table towards the bar area of the airport, and asked his Mum if it was okay to have a game whilst they were waiting. Mum glanced at Dad to seek some sort of approval and then nodded her head.

"Just stay in that area and don't spend all of your money," she said. She took the two suitcases and passports from the boys and moved up again in the queue.

Adam tucked his tee-shirt in behind his shorts and walked over to set up a frame of pool. Pool was one of Jack's favourite games. He used to play a lot when they had an old table over in Granny's shed, but unfortunately the table had become unplayable due to dampness.

Jack reached for the triangle from the compartment at the end of the table as Adam slotted in two coins and pushed in the silver lever to release the balls. The balls could be heard rattling out under the heavy slate table. Adam assisted Jack in setting up the pool balls by using the triangle to centre the multi-coloured group onto their correct spots.

"I'll break!" said Adam frantically, knowing that he would have to gain some form of advantage while playing Jack.

There was some dance music being played in the bar area which helped Adam get into the flow of the game by sinking a yellow-striped ball into a far corner pocket.

"Good shot!" said Jack. He appeared slightly stunned at Adam's sweet connection. "Hey, look over there!" he then whispered, observing a dog that slightly resembled Club.

The dog came to a halt and stood upright. It was a golden retriever and holding its leash was a woman wearing dark sunglasses. The dog sat up mannerly, allowing its owner to sit down on a chair. Its eyes stared up at the woman, making sure she was okay, and then it dropped its head to relax, not taking any notice of the surrounding commotion.

"That's a guide dog!" stated Adam. He bent down to align the white ball with one of the stripes.

"It's pretty amazing how well trained and disciplined they are, isn't it?" replied Jack, fascinated at its loyalty and respect for its owner.

Within seconds a well-dressed man dashed across the airport wearing a long black jacket floating out like a superhero's cape. Both brothers couldn't help but notice an envelope fall from his briefcase. The blind woman's golden retriever cocked its ears as it also witnessed the event.

Without hesitation, Adam and Jack jogged over. Adam picked up what looked like documents and accidentally allowed a piece of paper to slide out from inside an envelope. He saw a black-and-white picture of two girls. On top of the sheet it read 'Ghost Workers'. Not wanting to be nosy, Adam slid the sheet back inside the envelope and looked up to see where the man had gotten to.

Adam nudged his brother. Jack grabbed the documents and followed after the swooshing black jacket.

"Sir, sir, you dropped this!" said Jack, passing the man and holding the envelope out in front of him.

The man came to a sudden halt and frowned as he peered over his rather fancy glasses to inspect what Jack had.

"Oh… Oh my god, thank you very much, young man," he replied. The man looked both shocked and relieved.

"No problem, my brother and I… we saw you drop it while you were moving," Jack said.

"Thank you, young man. You're a good detective, we could do with you on some of our cases," he said. He held out his hand to shake Jack's.

Jack knew by this man's posture and by his overall demeanour that he held a position of some importance and felt he had really done his good deed for the day. He also noticed a badge of some sort inside his jacket when he stretched out his hand.

Jack then went on his way. He walked back to the pool table feeling good about himself and in some way feeling curious about this man he had just met.

The boys finished up their game of pool, Jack being the winner, and before long all family members were on board the flight. Mum took

out her library book and tilted her seat back
before she began to read.

"Ah yes, this is the life!" she exclaimed, relaxing
back in the seat.

Chapter 4 – The Flying Magician

The feeling on board the flight was one of great excitement. Everyone was eager to arrive at their destination and enjoy a much-deserved break. Adam was thrilled to be going abroad as he was ready to soak up as much information and knowledge as possible, which would help him with the geography curriculum next year.

The two female flight attendants were dressed in peach-coloured uniforms with white caps. Their make-up was peach-coloured too. The dark-haired girl demonstrated how the life jackets should be worn while the red-haired girl announced where the emergency exits could be found. Jack and Adam had been on a plane before, but still found this part of the proceedings of interest. They followed the flight attendants' actions and listened attentively. As the flight attendants explained how to use the seatbelts, the plane began to prepare for take-off.

The flight attendants took their positions in the stewards' cabin, strapping themselves in as the engines began to roar.

"Thirty thousand pounds of thrust per engine, boys!" said Dad, who had an interest in all things mechanical.

The plane lurched forward and pushed them all right back in their seats. The brothers peered out at the white lines on the runway until they began to disappear. As they continued to look out the window their stomachs began to feel heavier and the feeling of being airborne was obvious. They observed the runways of the airport and the surrounding roads, houses, shops and sheep in the fields that looked as if they were so close, but in reality were miles from the airport.

Within minutes, Jack became bored, now realising that he did not in fact have everything with him. Ironically enough, he had forgotten to bring his headphones. He scanned the area, wondering how he would pass the flight. Adam just sat back chewing his sweets, gaping out at the clouds that disappeared as the plane rose higher and higher into the clear blue sky.

On turning to his left, Jack saw a middle-aged man wearing a bright purple suit jacket and trousers. The man had slick, wavy hair and wore an earring in his right ear. Jack could not help but stare at this spectacle, as he was not a character you would spot strolling through Willows Town on a daily basis. He looked conspicuous and intriguing.

Noticing Jack staring at him, the man turned round and made a hand gesture.

"Hello!" he said in a deep voice. "How are you doing?"

Jack, now blinking to snap out of his trance, sat back in his seat and responded anxiously, "Hi, I'm fine thanks; just a little bored!"

"Do you like magic?" the man asked, now realising that all the family members were focused on him.

"Magic, yes I love magic," responded Jack. He opened his seatbelt with eagerness. The man reached inside his waistcoat and pulled out a euro coin. He opened both palms of his hands to show there was nothing in them and placed the coin on his left palm. He then folded his fingers, slowly enclosing the metal coin.

"What would be the most exciting thing I could do with this coin?" he asked Jack, who was now deep in concentration, not taking his eyes from the man's hand.

"Emm... make it disappear maybe?" said Jack, briefly looking up at his eyes to get some sort of a reaction.

"I can do better than that!" replied the man. He winked over at Dad, who was becoming rather interested, to say the least.

He opened up his left palm very carefully and everyone looked inside with great interest. They could see a small reddish piece of paper in the shape of a rectangle. Jack and Adam stared curiously as the man carefully opened up the piece of paper, showing its many folds and revealing more of what it was. Jack looked on in amazement as he recognised the paper as money. It was a ten-euro note. There was no sign of the previous coin anywhere.

"What?" Jack shrieked, his eyes wide with surprise, and then he burst into laughter.

"Now that's good!" Dad blurted out. He focused his eyes on the ten-euro note to see if it was real.

"Here, you can have this for your holiday," said the man. He held out the note to Jack.

Jack took the note, not knowing what to say. "Thank you very much, that trick was amazing," he said, swinging around to show it to Adam.

Adam was in a state of bewilderment. He initially thought he was seeing things when he found the coin had vanished, but then for it to have turned into money was a magic effect he had never experienced before.

"That's my lucky tenner now," muttered Jack. He held out his hand to introduce himself to the magic man.

"I'm Jack and this is my family. We all love magic!" he said enthusiastically.

"I'm Marcus, but my stage name is Eclipto," the man replied. He reached into his pocket once again.

"I'm a magician. I am travelling to Gallibar for a few shows," he continued.

Wow, Jack thought, a real magician! "I have never met a real magician before," he said, smiling up at his Dad in excitement.

Marcus pulled his hand from his pocket and

placed an unopened deck of cards on the tray table in front of him. Everyone could clearly see that the plastic seal was still on these cards and obviously it was a new deck.

"Have you ever seen any card tricks before?" asked Marcus, now getting into his routine, rubbing his hands together and stretching his fingers.

The only time any of the boys had any real dealings with cards was maybe at Christmas, when Granny or some other relations would pop around for an evening visit. Adam especially had always been fascinated any time a magician would call to their school to perform a magic show. Both boys now sat upright and focused on Marcus and his cards.

"I want you to think of any card from the deck and name it!" he explained to Jack, staring into his eyes.

Jack looked around hesitantly at the rest of the crew to seek some form of advice and then decided to choose the jack of clubs. Club, after his pet dog, and Jack, for his own name.

As Jack did so the man focused deep into his eyes. "Well, it's very strange that you have chosen this card," replied Marcus. He peeled the plastic back from the sealed deck. "It's strange because I actually felt you would pick this card and have deliberately placed it upside down in the packet," he concluded.

"No way!"Jack answered. He felt that this must be some form of joke.

All three fixed their eyes on Marcus's hands as he opened the deck and skimmed through the cards professionally. He kept a confident and charming smirk right across his face as he did so and the man next to him couldn't help but look in as well and watch all of this eagerly.

As he slid through each card, revealing the different suits and numbers, one card in the deck was turned upside down. Carefully he reached for this card and handed it to Jack. Feeling a little freaked out, Jack instantly flipped the card over and sure enough it revealed the jack of clubs.

"*Oh my God!*" they all cried out in shock, stunned at the talent of this man.

"How is that possible? The deck was sealed and unopened," cried Adam, his mouth wide open in dismay.

"Was it a guess?" asked Jack, still baffled.

"Well it might have been, but I can also get a good read on someone just by looking into their eyes," explained Marcus.

He turned slightly and looked into Jack's two wide eyes.

"For example, I can tell that you probably chose the suit, clubs, after maybe something that is black... or wait, maybe after the name of something... like a.... pet, maybe?" he asked.

Adam was taken aback by this statement, now more fascinated than ever.

"Yes... a pet dog maybe," said Marcus. He squinted his eyes as he concentrated harder. "But I feel that this pet is not quite happy at the moment, it's not its usual self?"

The two brothers stared at one another, wondering if Marcus was taking a wild guess or whether he knew something. Jack also began to wonder if his eyes were that readable. It was evident that Marcus was not just an ordinary magician.

"Yes, you are right, our dog Club was hurt, but can you tell us how she got hurt?" inquired Adam, now curious to see if Marcus could really read any more information from Jack's pupils.

Marcus then reached for his coat pocket once again, revealing three sealed brown envelopes. "I'll tell you what; you can decide the answer to that question. Inside these three envelopes there are three words written down on pieces of paper. Whatever envelope you pick, the word contained therein will reveal the answer. Here, choose one, but be careful!" instructed Marcus.

He fanned out the envelopes between his fingers.

Dad was now fully engaged, watching everything that was happening. Adam nervously reached out his hand to take the last envelope in the row.

"Ouch!" Adam cried. He felt a sudden burst of heat on his hand. It felt like his thumb and index finger were being burned, and he immediately dropped it.

"What happened?" asked Jack, looking at his brother in astonishment.

"It was hot, the envelope burnt me," he answered in confusion.

Marcus reached down and placed the envelope between his hands. He carefully and slowly ripped the seal, opening the envelope and revealing a piece of paper with the word 'FIRE' on it.

"Your pet dog had an accident with fire, isn't that right?" said Marcus.

Neither Jack nor Adam nor Dad knew what to say. Marcus had just taken the word 'magic' to a new level. They found his talent surreal and in some ways quite scary. They sat and chatted to him, learning more and more as their time on the plane flew by.

Chapter 5 – 'It's a Date'

When the stewardess announced that the plane would be arriving in Gallibar City within ten minutes, Jack wondered where the time had gone. He and his brother had had more fun during this trip than they had known all summer. Marcus had given the boys some special, almost secret, techniques to try on their friends, which they were eager to put into practice when they returned home. He had also explained the tricks he had done earlier. They were actually quite simple in theory, but lots and lots of practice was needed to perform them as well as Marcus.

Adam did not even notice his ears pop as the plane came to a standstill and everyone began the hustle and bustle of locating their baggage and passports for checking.

"Well, you two look like you had fun!" said Mum. She placed her library book into her bag and followed the boys down the steps into new territory.

"That was brilliant, he taught us loads of stuff!" answered Adam.

"Yes, I have to say he was as good a magician as I have ever seen," replied Dad, turning his head left and right to see where the airport exit was. Scanning for signs for the departing buses, the family eased their way out of the airport, clutching their belongings.

Adam immediately began to soak in some of the surroundings. The layout of the landscape looked quite different from that of home and it seemed a great deal busier than a typical Saturday morning back in Willows Town.

"We need to locate our bus to get to our hotel!" Dad announced. He took out a sheet of paper from his back pocket. "Come on, this has to be the one," he said, pointing to a large bus with crowds of people getting on board.

"These people must be going to the Old Town too," said Mum. She lifted up her bags.

"Old Town, Gallibar!" the man on the bus shouted out, giving a sharp glance at Adam's pale legs as he mounted the bus.

Dad smiled at the man as he hopped onto the

bus, thinking how convenient it was that English was also the official language in this country. Mum wished she had a pair of shorts on, as it was extremely clammy on board the full bus. Adam lifted his suitcase up into the overhead storage and glanced around for somewhere to sit. There seemed to be no vacant seats. All on board the bus were tightly packed together like sardines.

"You can sit here," came a soft voice from the back of the bus.

Adam tentatively turned around to see who was speaking. His eyes opened wide as he noticed two girls gesturing towards him to come over.

"Come on, there's room here!" one of the girls said, smiling and moving in closer to her friend.

Adam, a little nervy, slowly approached the girls and sat down on the space they had left for him.

"Thanks," he said, stealing a look at their two pretty faces.

They were the most gorgeous girls that Adam had even seen. They had two glamorous smiles and stunning clear skin. Both girls had long brown hair down to their shoulders and their bright blue eyes glowed.

"Hi, I'm Mia and this is Pippa. Are you on holidays?" asked one of the girls. She moved closer to Adam.

Adam pulled his body in, allowing a little room for Mia to sit over.

"Erm, yes," answered Adam, slightly stuttering. "Me and my family have just arrived, we're staying in the Old Town for a few days." He swallowed some saliva in his dry mouth, mostly from nervousness.

"Oh really? We live in the Old Town also. That's a great place to spend a vacation, you will have a great time!" said Mia. She looked directly into Adam's eyes and smiled.

"You will love it," added Pippa.

Each time the girls smiled or joked, Adam would briefly turn around and hope Mum, Dad or Jack would see him. He was revelling in each and every minute of the girls' presence. As Jack felt more and more claustrophobic squeezed in with his parents, Adam was gaining confidence and getting his holiday off to a wonderful start.

They chatted and laughed for the duration of the bus ride. Adam didn't want it to end.

"Right, this is the stop!" Pippa exclaimed. She packed a few of her things in her rather expensive-looking shiny red bag.

"Yes, I'd better be off," said Adam, still unable to take his eyes off the girls. He pulled himself up out of the seat.

"Well, maybe we can see you again and we can show you around the Old Town… if you like?" said Mia. She flicked her hair back.

Adam's eyes opened even wider upon hearing this and his ears perked up just like Club's would before receiving her dog nuts.

"Ah… ya, that would be super!" he answered, feeling ecstatic inside.

"Right, it's a date then, we can meet you in front of the Old Towers in the centre of the Old Town tomorrow at twelve," said Mia. She rose from her seat, exposing her own fancy handbag.

A date! Adam thought, re-joining the others, who now looked quite exhausted and jetlagged. He had a beaming smile right across his face.

"Hey!" Jack groaned, clearly groggy from the heat of the bus. "Why are you so happy?" he inquired further.

"Oh! Have I got good news for you, brother. I

have just organised two dates for us tomorrow," he said confidently. "I'll tell you all about it back at the hotel."

Chapter 6 – The Big Wall

Jack, Adam, Mum and Dad got off the bus and began to gather a sense of their new surroundings.

"Wow! There is so much to learn here, it's almost like we are back in medieval times," said Mum. She squinted her eyes as she gaped around the area.

"Yes! It's beautiful, very historic indeed," replied Dad. He dragged the heaviest suitcase up the cobblestone streets towards the hotel.

Adam had planned on taking notes and learning about the culture of the area, but now the only thing he could think about was Mia and her friend Pippa and meeting them by the Old Towers tomorrow.

They all approached the hotel they would be staying in for the next few days. It was very large and glamorous and the boys realised that their father must have spent a fair bit of money on booking it.

"Good choice, Dad!" Jack commented. He looked at a large fountain that decorated the reception area.

While Dad sorted out the hotel rooms and key cards, Jack bent down on his hunkers for a little breather. He imagined swallowing a nice chilling can of orange as he stretched his legs, allowing some of the blood to circulate.

"Room 107, boys, let's go!" Mum shrieked, all excited, collecting her key card and searching for the nearest elevator.

Adam and Jack tossed a coin to get choice of rooms. Adam, who was on a winning streak, was now the fortunate occupant of the large double bed overlooking the old medieval town.

He bounced up and down on the cool mattress as he sucked in the refreshing cold air from the air conditioning. Jack disappeared into his room to investigate while Mum and Dad pulled the surrounding curtains wide open for a look at the view.

"That must be it!" gasped Adam. He could see the top of an Old Tower up towards the centre of the town. He lay back on his bed, thinking about tomorrow.

Jack entered his room at a fast pace and quickly reached for his pocket to take something out. He tucked his hand neatly under one of his new pillows. He then opened his window to let in some fresh air.

Directly outside he could see a large concrete wall. The wall towered high up beyond his view. He looked back and forth, wondering what such a daunting wall was doing alongside such a classy hotel.

Soon they got showered and were now eager to check out this much-talked-about Old Town and get some food.

Chapter 7 – The Family Dines

The four, all neatly dressed in their holiday clothes, walked past new arrivals waiting to check in on the ground floor. The two electric doors opened wide in front of them as they stepped back out onto the streets of Gallibar and up towards the Old Town area.

"It's different," said Jack. He glanced at some of the medieval buildings and stonework.

Adam nodded his head in fascination. He could see the main part of the town just ahead with the many holidaymakers gathering about. He could hear the sounds of music in the distance where a performance of some sort was on. He also smelled the aroma of cooked food.

"Wow! Look at all the stalls!" cried Mum, eager to go over and start shopping.

Just as she moved forward she was rushed upon by a young child. It was a young girl. The girl instantly placed their hands in front of Mum and pleaded with her for some change.

She wore raggedy clothes and had a rather unpleasant odour. Dad stepped forward and placed a euro coin in her hand. The young child curled her fingers tightly around the coins and nodded her head frantically in to say thank-you. Jack and Adam looked on, feeling sorry for the girl as she dashed up the busy street and down a side alley. As the family carried on along the streets of Gallibar they began to encounter more young children out on the streets and in among the tourists, some not even wearing shoes, approaching strangers for anything they could spare.

Adam flinched as he passed a boy who could have been no more than seven years of age sitting in a shaded area just to the left of a sausage stall. He had nothing on but a pair of old shorts and his body looked thin and malnourished. To his side was an open plastic container with little coins inside. Adam put his hand into his pocket as he stood opposite the young boy and took out a two-euro coin. He carefully walked over and placed the money down into the container. The money made a little sound as it dropped inside and the boy peered out through his half-shut eyes. Jack too reached inside his pocket for some change and flicked it into the boy's container. Mum smiled at the kind acts of her sons but couldn't help but shake her head at the poor little boy's situation.

Dad continued to lead everyone up the main street and then suggested that they head into a side street. This street was narrow and the cobblestones were awkward to walk on.

"Aah! My friends, my friends, you eat? Sit down, please!" said a local man at the door of a small restaurant. He wore a rather old-looking suit and had his hair combed back over his head. He slightly startled the family but his warm smile instantly created a pleasant atmosphere.

He's a little over-eager, thought Adam, wiping his brow gently.

Before Dad even had a chance to respond, the man had placed his hand gently across his back and began escorting him towards a seat.

"Ah, okay," responded Dad. He looked back at Mum, who began to giggle.

"Sit down here, it's nice and cool," said the man. He indicated an area outside the restaurant.

A young waitress instantly arrived, greeting each of them with a warm smile, and placed several menus on the table. She could well have been the daughter of the man who met them at the door; her hair was dark and neatly tied back with little flowers along the side, stretching all the way to the back of her head. Her waitress uniform was simple but neat, with checked blue-and-white patterns along the front of her top, which hung slightly over her trousers.

"What would you like to drink?" she asked, taking out her little notepad and pencil.

"A jug of water is perfect thanks," replied Mum, deciding to keep it simple and save money.

"I'll have the chicken!" Jack blurted out. He wasn't too bothered about trying any of the other options.

"Yes, same here," said Adam, also wanting to play it safe and stick to what they were familiar with.

Dad decided to get some form of fish that was supposed to be extra fresh and tasty at this time of year.

"If Diamond was here I reckon she would order the fish too," remarked Adam. He pondered on how the two animals at home were coping and hoped Jasmine was treating them well. He also couldn't help noticing some of the animals he had passed by on the way down the street. Dogs and even some cats scrummaged about in many of the nearby bins in search of scraps. They didn't seem at all well, and like many of the street beggars and street performers they looked shockingly underfed.

It wasn't long before the food arrived via the smiling waitress. As Adam ate his portion of chicken, he thought about how he was going to ask his Mum and Dad about meeting the two girls the following day. He knew well that in a foreign country like this it would be quite dangerous to separate from his parents but he felt Mum and Dad accompanying him with the two girls would be a disaster.

All four were soon fed and the owner and waiter were very pleased with Dad's rather generous tip. Back onto the street they ventured, where crowds of tourists flocked up and down this relatively small town. Men and women were using large cameras to take photos of some of the ancient towers, red brick houses and medieval carvings. Business people stood outside each restaurant and shop, doing their best to entice groups inside to purchase some of their merchandise. Stalls were neatly set out throughout the market square, displaying a range of souvenirs, from knitted tea towels to novelty cigarette lighters. Mum was fascinated by the various nationalities of tourists around. Americans, French, Spanish and Germans walked through the streets, all keen to explore some of Gallibar's culture and heritage.

"Come on, I'll get some ice cream!" said Adam, approaching one of many stalls in the centre of the town.

The stall provided scoops of all flavours that you could imagine. Adam bought a double scoop of vanilla and strawberry with some of his money. He bought his brother and parents some scoops of the mint flavour. He sat down on a nearby bench and relaxed, taking in the magical surroundings. He scooped some of the strawberry ice cream up with the plastic spoon, allowing the flavours to melt in his mouth.

Chapter 8 – Rendezvous

The family arrived back at the hotel that evening after some monotonous shopping with Mum, who was as indecisive as ever, not able to decide which souvenirs to buy. Adam and Jack planned on togging out and jumping into the indoor pool on the ground floor.

"You will have to tell them soon," said Jack, flicking his ear to dislodge some of the water.

"I will after this," said Adam. He was hoping to put off the inevitable 'No, you have to stay with us' speech from his Mum.

The two brothers had the full pool to themselves. Jack always got bored with basic swimming and wanted to experiment with different activities in the water. He caught a few plastic floats that bobbled on the pool's surface.

"See if you can stand on them," Jack gestured to Adam. He flung three floats in his direction.

Adam shoved the floats down under the water and tried to keep himself up by standing on them like a surfer. The floats weren't that big, just a little larger than the length of Adam's feet. It looked quite silly from an onlooker's perspective but Adam had to admit it was quite fun when he started getting the hang of it.

They passed the evening playing about in the pool and ended up taking advantage of the free hot showers in the changing area. Jack closed his eyes and let the hot water seep through his skin, knowing that his mother would not be ordering him out of the shower this time.

Just before bed Adam became very anxious. He spent that night like a lot of nights before school on the Monday, except this time the circumstances were a little different. His head twisted and tossed on the pillow as he thought about meeting the two girls the following morning, hoping his parents would give him the thumbs-up.

"Right, I'm going for it!" he decided, getting up and approaching his Mum and Dad's bedroom the following morning. He eased his way over to the room and slid the door ajar.

"Dad!" he called out gently, waiting for a reply to see if he was awake.

Dad groaned, letting Adam know he could hear him.

"Is it okay if Jack and I meet up with a few friends this morning in the town?" Adam asked nervously. His heart was beating fast.

"Friends?"Mum replied, coming out of her sleep. "Which friends are these?" she inquired, lifting herself up in the bed.

"A few friends that I met on the bus, on the way from the airport. They said they will show us some cool sights in the Old Town. It could be very educational," replied Adam. He didn't want to disclose the fact that these 'friends' were two girls from Gallibar.

"Well, I want to have a look at these friends first. Don't want you hanging around with complete strangers!" Dad answered.

"When and where are you meeting them?" asked Mum. She reached for her dressing gown.

"This morning at twelve in town," replied Adam, feeling like this conversation was going just how he had foreseen it: dreadfully.

Adam advised Jack to wear his new tee-shirt and his good shoes for the day. Just like Jack, Adam got himself as spruced up as possible, wetting his hair, brushing his teeth and wearing his thick socks even though it was quite hot.

Adam, Jack, Mum and Dad walked down to the centre of the town early that morning. Adam tried to ease back and not walk directly beside his Mum and Dad in case the girls saw him. Jack seemed oblivious to the whole situation, not understanding at all what was in store for him during this 'date'.

"There they are, over there!" cried Adam. He gestured to his Dad to take a look.

"I don't see them!" exclaimed Dad. Hastily he moved his eyes around the vicinity.

"Those two, over there," said Adam, pointing his thumb in the girls' direction.

"The girls?" said Dad, puzzled. "You're meeting those two girls?" He sounded shocked.

"They are pretty," said Mum. She looked at them from the corner of her eye.

Jack stood staring directly at the two in awe and wonder.

"Okay, boys, we'll let you meet up with them

for a while, but we'll be in town also and we will join up with you shortly, is that okay?" Mum asked, understanding what it must be like for Adam and trying her best to be fair.

"Thanks, Mum!" said Adam. He took a deep breath before walking over and approaching the two girls, who waited by the high medieval towers.

"Hey!" Mia called out. Gently she opened her arms to give Adam a hug.

Adam, feeling slightly flustered and anxious, did his best to act calm and casual.

"This is my brother, Jack," he said, stepping back to allow Jack to shake hands with the girls.

Pippa had no time for handshakes. She gave Jack a large hug also. Adam smiled seeing the glint in Jack's eyes.

"There are many things to see here. We will go to an old medieval museum first, I think," said Pippa.

Jack and Adam felt like two celebrities walking up the cobbled streets with these two girls. Both girls were very well dressed in light summery tops and wore large, expensive-looking sunglasses. Their walk was brisk and efficient, showing clear signs they had followed this route many, many times.

The town itself was extremely busy, with crowds admiring the medieval gabled roofs and decorated high walls. Pippa led the way and brought the other three towards a stairway leading up to an old door.

"Welcome to the museum!" a Gallibarian woman exclaimed inside the door as she handed Pippa an information leaflet. "It's five euro for thirty minutes or ten euro for an hour. What you would like?" she asked.

"Umm, a half-hour is okay!" Pippa replied. She turned around to Mia, to see if that was okay.

"That will be five euro each please," said the woman on the door, holding out her hand for the money.

Pippa then eased back from the counter and glanced meaningfully over at the two boys. Not wanting to seem mean, Adam reached into his pocket and pulled out some money.

"Here!" he said, handing the woman four five-euro notes.

"Enjoy!" the woman exclaimed. She opened the door to allow everyone into the adjoining room.

Inside, the boys and girls met some other groups checking out an exhibition of old medieval equipment. There was a range of different weaponry on show, like battle axes and crossbows, which Jack particularly enjoyed. Ancient armoury hung on the walls and decorated the ceiling of the room.

"Wow! So much cool stuff here," said Adam, loving the fact that he could really learn from this experience.

"Check out this chair!" Pippa said excitedly, calling Jack over towards what appeared to be some form of chair that criminals of the past were executed on.

Jack's face flinched as he read the poster on the wall outlining its function and use. Pippa elegantly moved from item to item, keeping by Jack's side, as he read some of the little pieces of information about the tools and working utensils of the past. Beautifully designed pottery and household furniture took up a large section at the side of the room. It was a fantastic exhibition. As the half-hour passed, Jack and Adam began to get more relaxed and confident in the presence of the girls.

Upon stepping outside into the frantic streets, one of the nicest smells captured the attention of everyone. Mia and Pippa knew straight away it was the almond stall. This was a stall that sold fresh packets of almonds to give the tourists a taste of the Old Town culture. The stall-owner, dressed in a medieval-style red dress, offered Adam a sample of some broken-up almonds which smelled and looked mouth-watering.

"Wow! That's delicious!" uttered Adam after sampling one from the open counter. He tried to savour the nut as long as possible in his mouth.

"If only monkey nuts tasted like this!" he said, smirking over at his brother, who was practically a monkey nut addict at Halloween time.

"Let's get some ice cream," said Mia. She took out a little pocket mirror and glanced at her hair.

"My treat!" shouted Jack, going to a nearby stall and placing money on the small counter.

He handed the girls their ice creams and just as he did was surrounded by a crowd of young children. The children eagerly held up their hands in the air to ask for money.

"Please, please help us!" they asked in their weak voices.

Jack, slightly shocked, took a step back to observe the children in their tattered, dirty clothes. Mia immediately bent down almost like she had known one of the children and handed over her ice cream. The little girl hugged Mia and scampered off with the rest to sit and share the little meal.

"That was nice of you," said Adam. He too felt sad for these children.

Mia nodded her head and quickly took out her pocket mirror once again to fix herself.

Jack decided to buy another ice cream for Mia and all four parked themselves up on a nearby bench for a quick rest.

"Pippa and I were just thinking, we should check out the shopping centre, just off the Old Town," said Mia. She looked over to Pippa through the dark sunglasses.

Adam immediately checked his watch and remembered that he had been given an hour or so to meet back with Mum and Dad. Forty minutes had already passed.

But before consulting with Adam, Jack blurted

out, "Yea sure, let's go!" He rose from the bench and waited for Pippa to join him.

Chapter 9 – Leading Them a Merry Dance

Adam, not wanting to ruin the buzz of their excitement, got up hesitantly, trying to keep the date going. Mia put the end of her ice cream in the nearby bin and then reached for Adam's hand.

Adam began to break out into a cold sweat. She must really like me, he thought, hoping his hands weren't sweating too much with nerves. Glancing back, he could see that Pippa had done the same with Jack, walking closer than ever by his side, hands interlinked.

Jack too was experiencing a mixture of nerves and excitement. If only some of our friends could see us now, Jack thought. He wished he could see the look on Mr Atkinson's face.

Now both couples passed some advertisers dressed in medieval armour and carrying intimidating swords in their hands. Like loads of other business people, these men were trying to get tourists to spend money in their shops, stalls, museums, bars or restaurants. Adam and Mia crossed over a pedestrian crossing and into the vast shopping centre. Just like Mr Hartigan's and Mr and Mrs Pegs' shop at home, people could get practically anything they wanted in this building alone. There were clothes shops, hairdressers, sports centres and restaurants all inside.

"Wow! I love this shop!" stated Mia. She broke away from Adam's hand and raced over to view some of the dresses on display in one of the boutiques. She then made her way inside with the rest following behind.

Flicking through the many hangers, scampering from aisle to aisle, she came upon something that caught her fancy. She pulled out a sparkling red-and-white top and placed it against herself. "Oh Adam, this is so nice, don't you think so?" she asked, all giddy.

"Ya, looks lovely, really suits you," answered Adam, nodding approvingly. He wiped his sweating hands against his trousers, a little unsure of how to act in these circumstances.

"Oh, it's fabulous, would you get it for me,

Adam?" asked Mia. She turned around with the dress swinging close to her body.

Adam raised his brow and his mouth stood wide open. He had some money with him but if he kept spending he wouldn't have much left at all for the next few days. He was unsure what to do.

Then Mia advanced closer to him. "Please, Adam, I really like this… and I really like you," she said. She reached over and kissed him on the cheek.

Jack, noticing this, turned his head to check if he was seeing things. Adam froze to the ground, blushing as Mia pulled the dress back against her once again.

"Hey, Pippa, look what Adam is buying me. It's so beautiful, isn't it?" she added, grabbing the attention of her friend.

On hearing the word 'buy' Adam sunk his hand into his pocket to make sure he had enough money to pay for this dress. Then, in shock, he headed over towards the customer service desk.

Pippa rushed over to the jewellery stand where she held some of the sparkling earrings up to her ears, checking how she looked in the mirror.

Adam and Jack felt out of place in this section as they weren't your typical clothes shoppers. They had never really taken much notice of style and fashion logos, so watching these girls do their thing in the store was a new experience for them.

"Do you like them?" asked Pippa, swinging around showing them off to Jack.

"Oh yes. They're nice," he answered. He flicked his eyes towards Adam.

The two girls floated like bees over towards the next jewellery section with Mia holding the bag carrying the new dress Adam had just bought her. These shelves were decorated with the most expensive bracelets and rings you could imagine. Some were bright gold and others were silver and bronze. Mia took out one of the heavy bracelets and gently placed it around her wrist. Pippa did the same with a different type and admired it, twisting her wrist from side to side.

"Take a look in this mirror," Pippa insisted. She urged Mia to walk up towards a large mirror just at the entrance of the shop.

The two boys turned around and followed

them, not really too interested in this part of their date.

Suddenly, before the boys could even blink, the two girls had raced out of the store. The siren and alarm immediately sounded out and a security guard stormed towards the exit area. The girls were gone.

Jack and Adam looked at each other in disbelief. The security guard headed for the two boys and grabbed hold of Jack's tee-shirt, identifying him as one of the boys who had entered the store with the girls. Everyone in the shop stood staring at Jack and Adam.

What has just happened? Adam wondered, feeling uneasy.

He could not believe what was going on. The girls had just stolen two expensive pieces of jewellery and now he and his brother looked like they were part of this robbery.

The security guard pulled the boys quickly in through a door just next to the entrance. The room was empty except for some jackets and items of clothing that hung up on a clothes rack. Adam was pushed to the side, and Jack's shoulder banged into his arm. The man closed the door behind them.

"We just met them today! We didn't know they would do this!" Adam cried. He began shaking with fear.

"We did nothing wrong!" screamed Jack.

The big man wearing a leather jacket, peaked cap and security badge spoke in a threatening voice. "Explain yourselves before I call the police!" he said. He stared at the two frightened boys.

"We honestly just met those girls today and we came in here and they ran out, we didn't know they were going to steal," said Adam, panicking. He turned to his brother for some support.

"Yes! It's true! We thought they were nice but if we knew this would happen we would never have met up with them," Jack responded, breathing heavily whilst trying to keep calm. He could still hear the alarm outside and the sounds of commotion at the far side of the wall.

The security guard twisted his head back and forth, scanning the door area rather suspiciously.

"It's like this, boys. Those items of jewellery

were very expensive. We are going to have to keep you two here all day as an investigation, or else you're going to have to hand over some euro – to compensate, you understand." His tone of voice had become lower.

Jack and Adam calmed down slightly, noticing the change in demeanour of the security guard. They had done nothing wrong all day and didn't feel like handing over money for something that didn't really involve them. But the thought of having to stay here for hours and deal with foreign police was very unappealing. They had to be back with Mum and Dad inside the next five minutes and the last thing they both wanted was for their parents not to enjoy their holiday on account of their behaviour.

"I have only ten euro!" pretended Adam, reaching for his pocket. He carefully made sure he kept some of the other notes tucked down at the bottom.

Instantly Jack did the same, understanding Adam's strategy. He rummaged around, pretending he only had six euro.

"This is all we have, plus it wasn't our fault!" stated Adam. He placed his and Jack's money together and handed it over to the security man. The man reached down at the money and counted it out, checking over his shoulder now and again.

"This... this isn't enough!" he said, putting the money into his pocket. "There will be an investigation into this matter with the police after we examine the store cameras," he said.

He tilted his cap down over his forehead and told the boys they could go. Jack and Adam dragged themselves out through the door and out of the store. There were noises all around them but in their heads they could only hear a silence. Their brains recounted the events of the day and they tried to piece some of the puzzles together.

Not only had they nearly got arrested, but they had really thought the two girls liked them. A part of their hearts sank to their stomachs. As Adam eased his heavy feet out onto the hot cobbled streets of the Old Town, he felt a new low.

He and his brother walked silently for several minute back down the cobbled street.

"You know, Adam, I have a bad feeling about

that security guard. He looked awful dodgy, and putting our money directly in his pocket like that – I just don't know?" said Jack. He frowned up towards his brother as he walked. "Maybe we should have waited to talk to the shop owner," he added sensibly.

Adam looked at Jack. He realised that he was probably right and that they had just been fooled twice in one day.

Chapter 10 – Sleepless in Gallibar

Back at their hotel room neither Jack nor Adam wanted to say anything to either of their parents. They just said that they had had an 'alright' time, trying not to sound unlike their usual selves. Not wanting to seem suspicious, they both force-fed themselves dinner that evening: steak and chips, more swallowed than chewed. Mum kept reiterating how great a day she'd had looking at the shops and reading her book in the sun. Dad had bought some handy new gadgets for work, along with many souvenirs to bring back home.

The tone of the holiday had changed for the boys. They were both furious, at themselves and at the girls for doing this to them. The weeks of saving, doing the neighbours' lawns, cutting hedges and washing cars to earn money to go away, all more of less spent in one afternoon.

Even their minds had been messed with. They kept recounting the day's events over and over in their heads. Why would the girls do this? Was it just a coincidence Adam had met them on the bus? Both brothers tossed and turned, unable to sleep, trying to understand.

Chapter 11 – Operation Almond

Morning brought bright sunshine and all seemed new in the day, but the boys soon remembered the reality of their situation: they had been fooled and were both down money and only one day into their holiday. They didn't say much to their parents and even less between themselves.

"Mum… Jack and I want to go to the museum today, we passed it yesterday and would like to go and explore. Can we go on our own?" Adam lied blatantly to his mother, which was very uncharacteristic.

"Okay, for a little while, but come back before twelve and we'll all go on one of those tour buses to have a proper look round the area," she said out of the side of her mouth, applying the dark red lipstick in front of the hotel room mirror.

Jack looked at Adam. Adam looked at Jack, jerking his head towards the door as he picked up his sunglasses. Adam rarely gave him one of those looks. Jack knew Adam meant business.

They both headed to the museum and waited outside. There were even more people about and the weather was hotter than the previous day. Jack flicked the sides of his shorts over and over again as they kept sticking to his legs. Adam breathed in and out anxiously.

"What are we doing here?" asked Jack.

Adam looked at him, wide eyed.

"You'll see," he replied.

Jack didn't know what to think. Adam had never spoken to him like this before. He was a little confused.

The boys continued to wait, not even noticing a tour bus pass them by with the tour guide telling the tourists about the history of the town.

Some time passed, and then some more time passed. Jack grew uneasy, knowing his brother had a plan but not knowing what that plan was.

Then Adam tapped on Jack's shoulder. "Right, let's walk this way," he said sharply, eyeing something in his peripheral vision, his teeth gritted.

Jack looked back. He saw Pippa and Mia enter

the museum with a boy.

"Over here!" said Adam as they crossed the cobbled street. "Now, we'll stand here until they come out again," he explained.

Jack was beginning to get the idea now, but he left his brother to dictate proceedings.

Soon enough, after about a half an hour, the two girls left the museum with their new victim. He was a nice-looking boy, about their age, wearing jeans and a checked shirt. They walked either side of him, holding his hands as they strolled down the sidewalk.

"Look, they're wearing the bracelets," whispered Jack, seeing the gold bracelet that Pippa had taken a fancy to the previous day.

"You're right, they are," answered Adam angrily.

"Right. Keep calm, we can follow them from a distance," instructed Adam.

Right, thought Jack.

They managed to keep track of them as they walked innocently through the streets, passing some street performers juggling pins frantically up into the air. Adam kept his sights firmly on Mia, who occasionally tossed her hair to one side. She was laughing at whatever the boy was saying, seeming to find it funny. The trail continued to another street and then down an even narrower side street.

Soon the girls stopped outside a camera shop. They released their grip on the young boy's hand and pointed at all the elaborate cameras on display. Adam peered from behind a café sign slightly down the street, and saw the two girls and boy enter the shop.

"We have action," said Adam. His eyes followed the thieves right through the shop door. "Come on Jack!"

The boys stayed on the opposite side of the street so they wouldn't be spotted. They were both pumped with adrenaline and adamant to catch these crooks in the act.

"I've an idea," said Jack.

He sprinted down the street and approached an almond stall. Taking out all the money that he had left, he bought several giant packets of almonds. He then reached into his pocket before racing back to his brother, who was now crouched down next to a recycling bin.

"Here, Adam, I brought something with me. I

forgot to tell you about this," said Jack.

He slowly pulled out something from behind his back. Adam stared up at him, wondering what his brother was on about.

Jack showed him his slingshot. He tilted it to show the new design. "This was something I was working on in my room a few days back. I designed it to get at some annoying birds but I think it has suddenly found a better use," he added, smiling.

Adam frowned and shook his head, wondering how his brother managed to get this past airport security.

"Okay, when you see them make their move let me know. They won't get away from us this time," said Jack.

Adam put his thumbs up and continued to focus on the movement of the girls. He knew that Mia and Pippa would play the same game with this innocent boy, and when he least expected it, steal something from the shop and run. He waited several minutes as tourists and shoppers passed by, curious about what he was at.

"Ok, now!" shouted Adam. He stood up and began to cross the road.

Jack, who had the almond packets opened and ready, tossed their contents onto the cobbled ground. They scattered all across the front of the shop. He then loaded up a nice chunky almond into the elastic band on his slingshot.

Mia was first out, holding a brand new camera in her hand. She brushed against a tourist's shoulder as she turned up the street. Jack released his taut slingshot and fired the almond at Mia's leg.

Feeling the sting, she impulsively pulled back her leg, causing her sandal to slide on the almonds. Her body swayed backwards. She began to lose her balance. She then crashed to the ground. *Thump!* went the camera and smashed into pieces.

Pippa also raced out onto the street. Seeing Mia stretched out on the ground with the camera in bits, she tried to change direction and stumbled into a recycling bin, her dark glasses falling from her face.

As she tried to get back on her feet, Adam sprang into action, standing in front of her.

"You!"Pippa shouted, recognising Adam from the previous day. "You don't understand," she gasped.

"Come back!" roared the shopkeeper. He raced onto the street, just about keeping his balance.

"*Get outta the way!*" screamed Pippa, lashing out at Adam.

"Uhhhhh!" exclaimed Mia, trying to get past Jack, who blocked her way.

The shopkeeper caught up, accompanied by a security guard, and they took hold of the girls. Adam was separated from Pippa, and within seconds more adults arrived on the scene. They were men dressed in black suits. Adam wondered if they were the local police. They immediately showed their badges to the shopkeeper and security guard, who were still restraining the two girls.

Mia screamed and screamed and tried to release her hands from the shopkeeper's grip. Her hair was dishevelled and she looked to have hurt her arm in the fall.

"We didn't want to do this, he made us. He's making us all!" screeched Pippa. Jack and Adam could see that lots of local police had now arrived on the scene. They were all dressed in police uniform and looked quite intimidating. Unlike back home, they wore bulletproof vests and carried guns. The local police now began talking to the suited men and questioning the innocent boy who had been with the girls, as well as the shopkeeper.

Adam and Jack stood watching it all. A big commotion was unfolding. Tourists gathered in crowds to see what was happening, and several beggars got down on their knees to gather up the scattered almonds.

Jack noticed one of the suited men begin the conversation with the police by displaying his badge. As Jack looked closer he realised the man looked familiar.

"We saw him before!" Jack cried. He tipped Adam on the shoulder.

Adam stepped out a little over some crushed almonds and focused his eyes straight ahead. "The airport... the man with the passport... that's him!" said Adam.

"Come on, we'll tell him what happened," said Jack. He placed his slingshot back in his pocket and walked ahead.

Jack approached the man with caution. He looked very domineering and seemed to be having difficulty communicating with the Gallibarian police.

"We met you at the airport," said Jack. He hoped the man would remember him. "I gave you back the envelope. We helped get these girls. They scammed us yesterday."

The man's attention was grabbed and he stopped talking to the police. He blinked over and over again, looking at Jack.

"We know about these girls. They stole bracelets yesterday," added Jack, this time louder.

The man nodded his head and indicated for Jack to follow him. Adam followed too and the man led them to one side. He then hopped into an unoccupied police car and signalled that the boys should jump in the back.

Chapter 12 – Going Undercover

Jack and Adam felt quite nervous. They had never been in the back of a police car, never mind one hundreds of miles from home. Many thoughts churned around in their minds as they both stared at the suited man.

"What's going on?" asked Jack, looking at the time on the dash of the car.

"Yes, I do remember you," said the man. He closed the car door and turned back to the brothers. "You say you met these girls yesterday and they fooled you with their scam?"

"Yes," answered Jack and Adam simultaneously.

"And we knew they'd do it again so we tried to catch them today. That's when you came," added Adam.

The man took in what the boys were saying and nodded.

"I understand," he replied.

He then held out his badge. "My name is Agent Marque Marquez. I'm trying to get these girls too. I've been following them, as well as others, all around Gallibar." The boys sat still, seeing the seriousness in the agent's body language. "I'm here with a team to try and uncover a kingpin crime boss," he continued.

Adam shuffled closer to the agent. "Crime boss? How do you mean?" he asked.

"My team and I have been investigating all these robberies committed by thirteen or fourteen-year-old boys and girls in the country. The leader, known as 'Ghost', is reportedly responsible for it all. He runs an organisation where he gets girls and boys to reel in innocent tourists at the airports and use them to get money and commit robberies. I bet these girls pretended to like you and wore dark sunglasses. And did you also get caught by the fake security guard? Ghost also has some adults in his organisation that are used for this part of the scam," he added.

Jack and Adam looked at each other silently and then turned to the man and nodded.

"Yes, this has been happening for the past two

months now and the local police cannot catch this man."

"Why is he called Ghost?" asked Jack. He continued to concentrate on everything the man was saying.

"Our team has given him that name as whenever we seem to get close to him, he just vanishes," responded Agent Marquez.

"What about questioning the girls? Maybe they will tell you where he is?" asked Adam. He looked over his shoulder, wondering if the girls were still around.

The man just shook his head. "Unfortunately this is no good, we've questioned about a dozen of these girls before and each one is petrified to say anything. It's really not their fault, you see."

"How is it not their fault?" asked Jack.

The man took a long pause before answering.

"Take a look around the Old Town and you'll see so many homeless and young children that have nothing," Agent Marquez explained. "Poverty is a big problem here. Some areas are rich with nice hotels and fancy restaurants and then just alongside you have the slum areas behind the walls and people who haven't even a slice of bread. It's terribly sad."

Adam stood silent, piecing the puzzle together in his head. "So this bad guy Ghost is taking these children and getting them to do these things for him?" he said.

The agent nodded quickly. "Yes, and he gives them food and somewhere to stay in return. We have tried to explain to the girls that we understand and that we want to help, but they're all too afraid to give Ghost up."

Adam dropped his head in thought. He now felt different about the incident the day before. These girls were living in fear.

"What can we do to help?" asked Jack, now feeling angry.

"Ya, I want to help too," said Adam. "There has to be a way to find where Ghost is."

The man paused for a few moments in thought. He then turned his head, noticing a local police officer coming to the car.

"Buckle up, boys," he cried, as he reached for the keys in the ignition and started the car. He revved it loudly and sped out past the tourists and police.

"Where are your parents? I need to meet with

them first and then maybe there is something you two can help us with," said Marquez. He reached for his phone and began making a call. Adam and Jack strapped themselves in and felt their blood boil inside their chests.

"Our parents will be back at the museum. It's not far," said Adam.

The man nodded approvingly through the car mirror.

Jack and Adam sat still while the agent talked on the phone. They heard him speak about some items to be gathered together. Adam heard the words *wig*, *sandals* and *clothes* above the loud traffic, and like his brother he wondered what the agent was planning.

Sure enough, Mum and Dad were outside the museum. Mum was taking photos of the nearby scenery as Dad looked around, presumably waiting for the boys to emerge from inside the building.

The man introduced himself and spoke with Adam and Jack's parents. Dad gave the boys a stern look; Mum trained her gaze on the suited man as he spoke, a look of horror on her face.

The man commented on the smart thinking and quick action of the boys, pointing out that they had been a massive help so far. He then told them a little about why he and other agents were in Gallibar, and how Jack and Adam might be able to offer some critical help in finding the main leader.

"Yes, Dad, and we want to help," hissed Adam.

Agent Marquez tapped Adam on the back approvingly and called everyone in close. He then explained what Jack and Adam could do to help.

Dad raised his eyebrows when he heard what the man was suggesting, and just as Mum was about to give her input a black car approached. There seemed to be another agent inside, judging by the similar black suit and dark sunglasses. Agent Marquez opened the car door and reached in to take out a box. It was about the size of a small suitcase. The brothers locked their eyes on the box as Marquez slowly released the clip to open it.

He pulled out two long brown wigs of girls' hair, two pairs of large dark sunglasses and two colourful tops.

"All I need you boys to do is dress up in disguise as two girls. Pretend you're Mia and Pippa and try and see if you can get some information from any of the others working for Ghost at the airport. That's where they begin their approach on the tourists. We had teams go undercover before but our cover is always blown. You two are of similar age: I think it could work," explained the agent.

"No way!" gasped Mum, pulling her glasses down and making a stern face.

"Yes, that's perfect, we are the men for it!" cried Jack, hearing the word 'undercover' and getting all excited.

Adam looked at the long brown wigs and then back up towards the man to see if he was really being serious.

"Your boys will be safe. All we want them to do is try and find some of these girls at the airport and even get chatting to them. They can pretend they are working for Ghost as well. There might be a chance they will get some information about where the other members of this organisation are hiding" outlined the agent.

"But what if this doesn't work and the girls see

through these disguises? What then?" said Mum.

"I understand your concern, but your boys will be watched at all times, and I will have a team following and standing by to intervene if anything happens," said Agent Marquez.

Mum shook her head. Dad looked down at Jack and Adam. He saw that his two sons would be a good fit for this operation. Jack might even look good wearing the wig.

"We'll do it," said Adam.

He thought about all the girls around Gallibar who were being forced to rob and commit other crimes because of this man. He understood that he and his brother could be the exact ingredients needed to help unravel it all.

He reached for one of the wigs and put it over his hair, adjusting it until it felt right. He then placed the sunglasses over his eyes and around the back of the wig.

"Here, Jack, you try this tee-shirt, I think it's the best size for you," he said. He handed his brother the light purple top and put the other, green one on over his own tee-shirt.

Another agent then got out of the car and

handed the boys two handbags and two bracelets to match the appearance of the girls.

"We also need a camera," said Jack. "The girls would have stolen a camera if it wasn't for us stopping them earlier."

Agent Marquez took out his phone to make a call.

Jack and Adam fixed their new disguises, trying to make the tee-shirts fit comfortably. They could hear the agent talking to someone on the phone.

"Okay, the camera is on its way," Agent Marquez said.

Mum shook her head, wondering if this was all some form of joke.

"I want to be around at all times," said Dad.

"Certainly," answered Agent Marquez. "Now hop in the back of that car and Agent Wolff will fix you up some more."

Chapter 13 – Improvisation

Jack, Adam and Dad got into the car and shook hands with Agent Wolff. He too wore a dark suit and had a slick pair of sunglasses covering his eyes.

He slid out a tray of make-up and began to apply it gently to the boys' faces. Dad stared in disbelief as his two sons were transformed into what anyone would think were his two daughters. Agent Marquez sat in the driver's seat and explained that they were heading to the airport.

The closer the boys got to the airport, the more the reality of what was about to happen was sinking in. This was a dangerous adventure, and Jack and Adam wouldn't have their full team with them: Club and Diamond were miles away.

Agent Wolff handed the boys two pairs of girls' sandals, and as they arrived at the airport another member of Marquez's team pulled up and handed over a brand new camera.

"Just try and act like two girls, you'll do fine," said Agent Marquez. He looked back over his shoulder to make sure he wasn't being followed.

"And remember, if anything goes wrong they will step in," added Dad nervously.

Jack and Adam nodded and got out at the clammy airport. They hadn't expected to be here again until they were going home. From head to toe they looked like girls. Jack had gone from hoping Mr Atkinson could see him walking down the streets with Mia and Pippa to praying no one he knew could see him now.

Jack held the camera in the way Pippa did and walked with a little swagger towards the main airport door. He and his brother were passed by families and couples flocking in for their holidays. Adam noticed a young boy his age standing next to his Dad, looking around and wondering where to go.

"Okay, maybe we should just wait here and keep a look out for some other girls," said Adam.

"Ya. Eyes peeled, they could be anywhere.

Remember they were on the bus when they got you," said Jack.

Adam nodded. He stood next to a drink machine wondering if it would be okay to get something to cool him down. The wig hung down to his shoulders and made him feel quite claustrophobic. They both stood there for about five minutes observing everyone that passed and trying not to look conspicuous.

The dark glasses made everything appear so shady and unclear that Adam tilted his pair down so that he could see properly. His eyes stopped at a poster which was an advertisement for Marcus's magic show.

He continued to look at the picture, reflecting on his meeting with the magician on board the plane.

"Wait a second, see them over there," hissed Jack. He tapped Adam on the shoulder. Adam forgot his daydream and came back to the present. He looked to his right and saw three pretty girls standing by the airport exit. They were scanning everyone that passed by. "See the handbags, and look how they're watching everything. They're definitely girls like Mia and

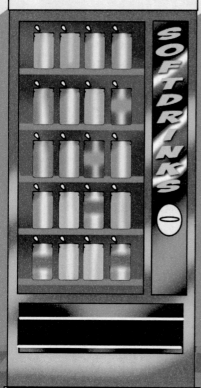

"SATELLITE STAN" DESIGNED BY WILLIAM HOBAN

Pippa," cried Jack.

Adam nodded his head.

He studied the girls for a minute. They definitely gave the impression they were looking for some tourist boy to break away from his parents so they could begin their scam. He thought about how foolish he must have been to be caught by this trick. Then he began to remember some other tricks he was taught the previous day, by Marcus. Maybe he could put some of these tricks to use to beat the girls at their own game. He started to imagine what Marcus might do in this situation.

"I'll take the camera, I'll do the talking," stated Adam. "Just go with my lead." He reached into his pocket for his last ten-euro note. He took a deep breath and walked in the direction of the suspicious girls. Jack followed, his legs feeling rather shaky.

Adam fixed his glasses and hair to make sure he looked okay. He knew that these girls mightn't even know who Mia and Pippa were as there were probably loads of people working for Ghost, so he and his brother could just try and pass as two other girls who were also part of the organisation.

As Jack and Adam moved closer, one of the girls turned towards them.

"Hey, ya get on okay? Look what we got," said Adam confidently, trying his best to sound like a girl. He held the camera up in front of the three. He then placed it in his handbag.

"So come on, how did your day go?" asked Adam, flicking his hair back and releasing a smile. All three girls looked confused.

Adam then raised his right hand up in front of the girls and waved it back and forth, keeping his thumb pushed in tight to his palm. He then reached in behind one of the girl's ears. In his hand underneath his thumb was the folded-up ten-euro note. Adam kept his eyes on the nearest girl and pulled back his right hand, this time in a fist, holding the ten-euro note. His hands were sweaty, but he had still managed to allow the note to come out from behind his thumb, creating the illusion it had just appeared from nowhere, or behind her ear. He slowly uncurled the palm of his hand just like Marcus had done and revealed the balled-up money note inside.

"I'll tell you what, you can tell us all about it over some ice cream when we go back," he said. He smoothed out the ten-euro note using his two hands before placing it in the girl's handbag.

All three girls stood still and smiled. They looked impressed. Jack smiled from under his disguise. He understood what his brother was up to. Marcus had taught them on the plane how tricks can be used to break the ice, to get into people's heads by not allowing them time to think; how it was important to keep talking and take the initiative when performing. Adam was putting some of these methods into action and it seemed to be working.

The three girls looked at each other and nodded. "Okay, let's go," one of them said. They placed their bags around their arms and began walking out of the airport doors with Jack and Adam.

Adam led the way, checking his sunglasses were in position and fixing his hair. He hadn't a clue where he was going, but just like Marcus had showed them with the card tricks he knew he had to go with the flow and improvise.

Jack knew the plan now and kept out in front

alongside Adam, pretending they knew where to head. He delicately swayed his bag back and forth like a teenage girl.

"The bus is over here. Where are you going?" asked one of the girls. She came to a stop and stared at Jack and Adam. Adam came to a halt and flicked his head around. His heart pounded and his mouth began to dry.

"Yayaya, we know we know, we were just wondering if we could fit in a quick robbery. There's a boy on his own up ahead, but ya, we'll leave that until tomorrow," he replied.

Jack shot his eyes at Adam, holding back a laugh. He then steadied himself and kept behind the girls with his brother as they boarded a shuttle bus.

The bus wasn't as busy as before so Jack and Adam sat just behind the three girls, hoping they wouldn't turn around and engage in any more conversation. Jack looked out the window hoping Agent Marquez and his team were close by. He knew this wasn't part of their plan.

He looked around and noticed a young family sitting just up ahead of him. One boy, presumably the youngest in the family, was sitting on his own on the front seat. Within seconds, one of the girls had left her seat and approached the young boy, sliding into the seat to chat to him. She twisted her hair back and forth in an effort to flirt with the boy.

Adam turned to Jack, wondering if he should do anything, but banished the thought. Anything they did now could destroy this whole undercover operation. Jack shook his head in dismay. These girls were not going to miss any opportunity.

As they watched from their seats, the girl continued to chat and laugh until the bus came to a stop. One of the other girls then rose from her seat and looked back at the brothers. Jack and Adam followed her out of the bus and back onto the streets of Gallibar. They walked in the direction of the shopping centre the boys had been in the previous day.

Like Jack, Adam was beginning to get a little worried. The further he went with these three random girls the closer he got to potential danger.

They were led inside the shopping centre, past the majority of shops and out onto the stairways and lift area. The girls then looked around to make sure they weren't being followed and then pushed the lever opening an emergency exit down one flight of stairs. The door led them underground towards the car park. Jack and Adam followed anxiously as they walked towards another door. It was quiet and eerie down here. There were one or two cars around but mostly just cold darkness.

Jack thought about it. People obviously didn't use this underground car park and it was close to the shopping centre. All the stolen goods could easily be brought back quickly and hidden. With no signs of any cameras, it was a perfect location for the gang, and was right under the authorities' noses.

As they walked through this next door Jack stood in a puddle, splashing cold water up into his sandals. His breathing got faster and he tried to settle his nerves.

Before them was a dark tunnel with only a thin light at the end. The girls walked on ahead, giving the impression they had done this trek a thousand times before.

As they walked, Jack and Adam could hear

some form of activity. They soon came out into a large open area. It was like an abandoned warehouse. There were no windows down here, just a few doors, and the place was lit up by hanging rectangular lights. The sight of the place sent a chill up Adam's spine.

In front of them was a crowd of about a hundred people. Some were girls, some boys and there were a few adults among them. Nobody even noticed the five enter the area.

The three girls then broke away from Jack and Adam and joined some others around one of the many tables. Adam watched on as one of the girls threw down a new watch to join what appeared to be another twenty or so stolen watches already there. As Jack moved forward a little, trying to keep calm, he could see thousands of euro worth of stolen goods scattered about on many tables, while lots of people stood around them sorting the items out. These people were children around their own age. They looked very tired and afraid. Some tables held expensive-looking bracelets and jewellery while other areas displayed large amounts of cash. The children were sorting all the stolen items and counting cash, while others seemed to be breaking up laptops and other devices.

Jack and Adam looked at each other through their sunglasses. They realised that they had more than likely discovered one of Ghost's lairs.

Jack looked around the perimeter of the warehouse. There were some scary-looking adults who were watching the girls and boys sort the different items while they held guns up to their chests. Some had dark beards and shaved heads, while others wore baseball caps angled down to cover most of their faces. As Jack looked across he made eye contact with one of the guards. He looked very similar to the fake security guard that had scammed them out of money the previous day. The man kept his eyes on Jack for a few seconds and began to walk forward.

"I think we've done enough. We should get out now. If we're caught we're dead," said Jack frantically.

Adam nodded. He looked for the door, getting ready to leg it. But as he did so the place was suddenly silent. Everyone stopped what they were doing, stood up straight and directed their eyes towards a door that was beginning to open. Adam stopped and the two brothers watched as the door slid inwards and a figure was revealed. It was a man. To Adam's eyes he looked quite normal. He had a black tee-shirt and longish blond hair covering some of his face. His sleeves were rolled up and there were tattoos covering his arms. Judging by the way the room maintained its silence and the way in which the man scanned the area in front of him, Jack could tell this individual was either feared or greatly respected.

"Is that him?" whispered Adam. He didn't turn his head for fear of being spotted. Jack made no response.

The man walked around the top of the room, observing the items that were being sorted, and looked a few of the workers in the eye. These people stood stiff and upright; some held their breath, while others seemed to tremble slightly as the man approached.

The man stood for several seconds, in silence.

"It has just came to my attention..." he breathed, "that two of our girls were caught today by the police." The man then stopped and looked round the room. His face didn't reveal any emotions but both Jack and Adam could feel the tension build.

"Remember, I have eyes and ears everywhere in this town." He paused once again. "I just hope they don't say anything to the police. For their own sakes," added the man in a sarcastic tone. He smiled cruelly to some of the armed guards. "Remember, I feed you all and give you a bed, don't ever forget that. Don't ever forget that," he repeated, raising his voice.

Again there was a moment's pause.

"I'd now like to introduce two new members to our organisation. Come on in, girls," said the man. He tilted his head and looked towards the door he had come in through.

Two girls walked in with their heads down, visibly tired and weak. They wore dirty old clothes and had some cuts and bruises around their knees.

"Lift your heads up when I am speaking to you!" shouted the man.

"Yes, boss. Yes, boss," the frail-looking girls replied.

Adam looked on and began to shake. He heard the word "boss" and knew this must be the bad guy the agent had told them all about. This must be the guy that was using all the innocent children around Gallibar. This must be…

Ghost.

Jack couldn't stop his legs shaking.

"You two will do fine. Good girls," said Ghost. He patted both girls on the tops of their heads. He then looked out onto the large group of workers and focused his gaze in Jack and Adam's direction. His head didn't move. He continued to look at the brothers. The boys knew he was looking at them.

"Why are you still wearing sunglasses?" asked Ghost.

Everyone in the room turned towards where Jack and Adam stood near the end of the room.

"Why are you two still wearing sunglasses?" he asked again, this time much louder. Jack and Adam only noticed now that everyone else in the room had taken off any accessories they had been wearing. They hadn't taken off theirs. As the room was quite dark they looked strange with their big sunglasses on.

The brothers turned to each other, wondering what to do. Their breathing accelerated and their bodies shook in fear. They could see Ghost move from his spot and make his way towards them.

Jack moved his shaking hand up towards his glasses and slowly took them off, flicking some of the hair of the wig across his made-up face.

Adam began to panic. He had had enough. He wanted out. He tried to move his hand and remove his glasses like his brother but his arm wouldn't move. It was frozen solid in terror. Noticing this, Jack reached across for his brother's glasses and removed them. Still everyone in the room stared in the boys' direction.

Ghost frowned. He was getting closer, moving between the tables where the stolen jewellery lay. The boys could feel his presence more strongly with every step.

Jack nudged Adam. He knew their cover was about to be blown.

"*Get out! Out! Out!*" he cried at the top of his lungs. He prayed the agents were somewhere close by.

Adam raced towards the door. Jack saw Ghost open his mouth and wave his hands about. The adrenaline was pumping so fast inside his body he couldn't hear anything. He raced for the door and darted out through it with Adam.

Adam could hear mayhem inside and the sounds of feet chasing after him as he tried to navigate his way back through the tunnel and find the outside door he had come in by.

Just as he made his way to the top of the tunnel a light shone in as the external door was opened and suited men charged through. Adam was thrown to the ground. His head hit the cold concrete floor and immediately he pulled himself back up.

A swarm of armed men bombarded their way in and Adam covered his face, praying for his life.

Jack too was thrown to the ground as the men raced past him towards the inner door.

"Adam, are you okay?" asked a voice.

Adam had fallen but the wig had protected his head from a bad bang. He looked through his fingers and saw Agent Marquez standing in front of him.

"It's okay, Adam. You're okay now," said Agent Marquez.

Jack made his way up through the tunnel and helped his brother up from the floor as more agents piled their way inside.

They heard gunshots, and then they were led by one of the agents out into the car park towards safety. As Adam reached the car park he noticed a black car speeding off. He could hear the screech of the tyres and guessed this was one of the bad guys getting away. The agent left the brothers to follow the car, so Jack and Adam continued through the car park door and were soon back in the shopping centre.

Jack threw his wig to the floor. He was sick of wearing it.

At once Adam saw Dad pacing back and forth. He ran up to give him a big hug. He couldn't remember the last time he had hugged Dad. It wasn't really his style, but on this occasion felt so glad to be back with him. Dad hugged the boys back, shaking his head, with a look of relief on his face. He understood now that this whole idea had been bad and was so thankful everyone was back safe.

"Okay, lads, if your Mum asks, don't go into too much detail," he said.

The boys nodded their heads and gradually their hearts settled back to their usually beat.

Agent Marquez returned, wearing his bulletproof vest and dark glasses. He was soon joined by the other agents who were bringing the criminals out. Two men came first, both handcuffed and one bleeding from the chin. The other's tee-shirt had been ripped and he shouted insults towards the agent escorting him. Jack and Adam raised their heads as the men passed, trying to spot Ghost. Soon the young girls and boys were brought out. They too were under arrest, but their faces had a look of freedom.

"Come on, boys, let's get you all back to your hotel. That's a great job you've done today," said Agent Marquez.

"Did you get him?" asked Jack eagerly.

"There are agents chasing him down now. He escaped in a car but we'll get him," Marquez answered. "Thanks to you we've uncovered one of his lairs and we have made some key arrests," he added.

The boys and their Dad were brought safely out of the shopping centre and returned, exhausted, to their hotel.

Chapter 14 – Last Request

"I can't wait to go home and wear my yellow jumper again," said Adam, firing all the girls' clothes off himself.

"Damn right," said Jack. He pulled and tugged at his face in an attempt to get all the make-up off.

Dad stood inside the kitchen explaining everything to Mum.

The holiday had been turned upside down, but the brothers still had a few more days to soak up the scenery and revel in the fact that they didn't have to do any housework and could enjoy swims down in the pool for as long as they liked. Dad had called home and found out that Club and Diamond has been a little lonely at first but were now enjoying the good weather and playing with a new toy that Jasmine had given them.

The following day, as the family sat down in the

place where they had eaten all week, Agent Marquez approached, this time dressed quite differently from before, in a casual shirt and a pair of jeans. He still wore his secret agent-style glasses, however, which was the first thing to capture the boys' attention.

"Good afternoon," he said. He pulled out a chair and shook Dad's hand. "I thought I would stop by and tell you the good news." He smiled at Jack and Adam.

"Good news?" asked Adam. He stopped chewing his chicken and gave all his attention to the agent.

"Yes," answered Marquez. He paused. "We found Ghost. Our team chased him in the car and he tried to get away to another one of his lairs. The team pinned his car in. There was a shootout and he was shot."

"Shot!" gasped Jack. "Was he killed?"

The agent shook his head. "He survived. He's in hospital now and when he has had surgery he'll be taken to jail."

The boys were silent, processing this new information.

"I cannot thank you enough. You don't know

how much of a help you were," said the agent. "And how you got the girls to bring you back, that was such skill. Our team is still talking about it." He reached and took his glasses off. "Is there anything I can do to repay you?" he asked.

Jack and Adam looked at each other and both knew what the other was thinking. "There is one thing that we would like," said Adam. His heart throbbed as he took a breath before asking. "We'd like to get a chance to see Mia and Pippa again before we go home." He turned to his brother to look for agreement.

"Ya, even just for a few minutes," said Jack.

The agent stood still, looking at the boys. He appeared a little shocked at the request. Adam knew he probably expected him and his brother to ask for money or even some cool gadget from the agency, but he felt that getting a chance to chat once again to these girls would be worth more.

The agent put his glasses back on. "Okay," he answered. "How about now?"

Adam slid his plate to one side, indicating that his dinner was finished, and Jack did the same.

Mum released a smile for the corner of her mouth at her two sons' enthusiasm. She looked quite proud at what her sons were asking for.

All the family sat inside the agent's car and were brought out of the Old Town. They stopped after about ten minutes of driving in a residential area. The houses were far from pretty. The windows were tattered and numerous items of rubbish lay tossed about.

Marquez explained that this was where Mia and Pippa, along with some other boys and girls, were now living. He explained that lots of the town's shops had donated the stolen goods to a fund that was going to be used to do all of these houses up and help make the area more homely and safe.

Jack hopped out of the car following the agent into one of the houses, feeling somewhat anxious. Adam was feeling even more so. He passed by a rather large stray cat that sat by the step.

Inside, the family could see lots and lots of boys and girls gathered round a large table. There was a smell of food and Jack and Adam could see that they were all about to tuck into a nice

Gallibarian meal.

All the children gazed over as the family moved towards them, led by the agent.

"Hey!" came a voice from across the room in an excited tone. Jack noticed a girl getting up from the table. She was soon joined by another girl. It was Mia and Pippa. Mia held out her hand to shake Adam's, who began to blush.

"Can we start over?" asked Pippa in a delicate voice. She too raised her hand to meet Adam's.

Jack held out his hand to shake Pippa's and stared into her face. Without all the make-up and fancy clothes she looked even prettier.

The boys sat down with the two girls and chatted about what had happened. Adam and Jack now understood the circumstances that led to everything, and were happy that Mia and Pippa were now safe and able to live a better life. They also began to realise how lucky they were to have such a nice family to bring them up and even bring them on holidays.

"You should see our dog at home, you would love him," said Jack, smiling from ear to ear and thinking about how Club would jump all over her.

"Ya, and we have a pretty cool treehouse too. We spend a lot of time there and think of really good things to do," added Adam, enjoying every second of the meeting.

The time soon passed and Agent Marquez returned and told Jack and Adam to follow him back to the car. Jack handed over his slingshot to Pippa as a present and pointed out that she could have this in case any bad guys ever tried to bully her again. The boys shook the girls' hands once again, and smiled.

As Jack began to walk away he stopped and turned.

"Maybe sometime you can come to our country and we'll show you around," he exclaimed. He turned to his brother.

"It's a date," added Adam, and all four burst into laughter.

THE END

Books in *'The Adventures of Jack and Adam'* series

For more information on 'The Adventures of Jack and Adam' series, please visit us on <u>www.jackandadamadventures.com</u>